The Lily Pad and the Spider

The Lily Pad and the Spider

Claire Legendre

Translated by David Homel

ANVIL PRESS • CANADA

Copyright © 2020 by Claire Legendre
Translation copyright © 2020 by David Homel

The Lily Pad and the Spider was originally published in 2015 by Les Allusifs under the title *Le nénuphar et l'araignée*.

All rights reserved. No part of this book may be reproduced by any means without the prior written permission of the publisher, with the exception of brief passages in reviews. Any request for photocopying or other reprographic copying of any part of this book must be directed in writing to Access Copyright: The Canadian Copyright Licensing Agency, One Yonge Street, Suite 800, Toronto, Ontario, Canada, M5E 1E5.

Library and Archives Canada Cataloguing in Publication

Title: The lily pad and the spider / Claire Legendre ; translated by David Homel.
Other titles: Nénuphar et l'araignée. English
Names: Legendre, Claire, 1979- author. | Homel, David, translator.
Description: Translation of: Le nénuphar et l'araignée.
Identifiers: Canadiana 20200302418 | ISBN 9781772141528 (softcover)
Classification: LCC PQ2672.E38 N4613 2020 | DDC 843/.914—dc23

Cover design by Rayola.com
Interior by HeimatHouse
Represented in Canada by Publishers Group Canada
Distributed by Raincoast Books

The publisher gratefully acknowledges the financial assistance of the Canada Council for the Arts, the Canada Book Fund, and the Province of British Columbia through the B.C. Arts Council and the Book Publishing Tax Credit.

We acknowledge the financial support of the Government of Canada through the National Translation Program for Book Publishing for our translation activities.

Anvil Press Publishers Inc.
P.O. Box 3008, Station Terminal
Vancouver, B.C. V6B 3X5 CANADA
www.anvilpress.com

PRINTED AND BOUND IN CANADA.

In April 2013, Jean-Marie Jot, the publisher of Les Allusifs, a French-language house, asked me to write something for a collection called "Les Peurs" — Fears. There were no formal requirements. The book just had to be short. It could be a story, an essay, brief inquiries, a kaleidoscope ... and it had to talk about fears. I began to study my own, systematically, to understand them and see what could be said about them. The collection no longer exists, but this little book lives on.

—*C. L.*

> As I take great pleasure
> in the present moment,
> I cannot vanquish
> the disorder that arises from the depths of my soul.
>
> —André Breton, *Arcane 17*

Tragic Irony

Hypochondria is an underground malady, largely unseen, relegated to the realm of the invisible by the symptoms it borrows from fatal diseases. The hypochondriac has chest pains. Essentially, that is where they are located (and where the name comes from, literally: under the cartilage of the breastbone). He feels other pains that are just as persistent, but this one is by far the most shattering. Because the hypochondriac knows that in his chest lie his lungs and to the left, and a little lower, his heart. The needles that seem to be jabbing between his ribs, the vise that seems to be compressing his thorax, keeping him from breathing deeply, they announce the beginning of the imminent and definitive end. The hypochondriac will treat his stomach pains with great contempt, since the stomach is not fatal (at least not in the short term), and he will look down on any mechanical irregularities in his arms, legs, back, etc. But the slightest soreness in his chest will set his head spinning with morbid ideas. He knows all is well; the last electrocardiogram made that clear. The examination of his respiratory system revealed normal functioning despite the daily pack of smokes he goes through with delicious guilt. But something stronger and more profound is happening. His worries are the guarantee that he will escape, *in fine*, all the ills the world holds. Accustomed to worrying for no good reason, the day he stops worrying, the tumour will creep into his chest. That tumour, that blocked artery, that imaginary aneurism – there is something intolerable about their virtual nature. He could not stand to be colonized from within, and not know it.

Those who suffer from phobias understand that the presence of the spider in your room is far more terrible than the spider itself. I have lived in countries where spiders are more sacred than cows in India because they are supposed to bring good luck, and I can tell you this: the most abysmal thing about spiders is that they were there the whole time you thought you were alone. You thought you were safe in bed, or that your mind was free to wander as you sat in your office, and suddenly you realize the cursed spider was sizing you up the whole time with its malicious eye, like a well-placed webcam it slipped into your privacy and you never knew it. Once you have crushed it against the white wall, the panic over the spider will send you on a frenetic search in case, by some chance, her sisters might be tormenting you from another spot in the room. Because there is something worse than being colonized by a spider – or a tumour – and that is not knowing you have been infiltrated. To be the butt of a cosmic joke. That spider, this tumour, they are God's eye. In Greek theatre, that is called tragic irony. You know, poor Oedipus promising to dispatch his father's murderer… The audience knows he killed Laius… He is the only one, poor fool, to remain ignorant. Hypochondriacs, like arachnophobics, fear the trap of tragic irony more than anything else, like Oedipus' final vexation as it closes around him. Instead of enjoying the moments of serenity that remain before the spider slips into his room, or the rival into his bed, or the tumour into his chest, the hypochondriac prefers to make the first move against the parasite, in order not to be surprised when it shows up. The hypochondriac fears nothing more than being caught off-guard. In a mad attempt to master his fate, and parry the blows that must come, he will pay for the sin of pride his whole life. In his moments of lucidity, and they do exist, he will admit that as long as he can spend his time inspecting the walls – or his wife's cell phone – and the condition of his ribs, he will have no other worry than the anticipation of future worries. Hypochondria, ironically enough, is actually the likely symptom of objective peace of mind.

The Prophecy

It was supposed to end July 3, 2007. That had been decided long before. More than once, and meticulously so. The idea came from childhood. From school. When I was nine or ten. I had a friend, I forget her name, a little gypsy girl who came in the middle of the year, she was very nice, and could read palms. I liked that because my grandmother read our Tarot when she wasn't interceding on our behalf at church, she prayed novenas, kept a candle lit for nine days, almost burning down the apartment, consulted a fortune-teller when necessary, and took me to Sunday mass the other times. Once a year we went to see Saint Anthony in Padua and brought back large plastic containers full of water from Lourdes that we drank to protect our health and make our prayers come true, our wishes, our desires, all synonyms for the same thing. That was my grandmother's way of loving us, with all her benevolence she communicated on our behalf with the forces that make decisions: gods, saints, planets, cards, pendulums, black cats, and hats absent-mindedly and unfortunately left on beds, mirrors tragically broken, and worse, the very worst, the neighbour lady who had the nerve to greet us in the morning with a "Good day!" that would bring bad luck, we had to do everything possible to avoid her completely, or as much as we could. One day my grandmother asked her to stop wishing us a good day, and I would have given anything to see the neighbour's face then or, better still, a few weeks later, when the words crossed her lips again. *Good day, excuse me.*

The little gypsy girl read palms and I don't know what romantic little game, ill-conceived or perverse, led her to announce one day, in the playground, that I would die at age twenty-seven. I was not overly concerned. Twenty-seven is a world away when you are nine or ten. Early death was a way of escaping old age, no one would see me with faded beauty behind my lace. It was almost flattering with its rock star feel, she added me to the list of the twenty-seven club with Jim Morrison, Hendrix, Janis Joplin, long before Cobain and Winehouse joined. I was ready for that.

There was nothing tragic about the prediction, and I didn't mention it to my mother. Even then I understood that at age twenty-seven, a person doesn't die of a disease. I knew I would escape death by overdose because, after the presentation the volunteer from the prevention centre gave us at school, drugs weren't my thing. At twenty-seven, a person dies in an accident. The idea, both nebulous and very clear, took hold in me: I would die in a car wreck at that fateful age.

I never got my driver's license.

When I was thirteen, the Oliver Stone film launched a very convincing Doors revival. I spent my weekends in smoky bars, smoking and listening to blues bands playing ecstatic and melancholy tunes (sometimes one, sometimes the other, sometimes both). That was when we fomented our project, Lisa and I. Lisa was my best friend. Same blond hair, same green eyes, but much more petite and cute and pretty than I was, which accentuated my awkwardness, my skin that refused to glow, my thighs that kept expanding. Her skin, as she grew older, would stay smooth, and when she opened her thighs they would be svelte. The boys used to ask me if I was chaperoning my little sister, and that was my only revenge since it drove Lisa crazy.

To tell the truth, that wasn't my only revenge. Lisa was probably more lost than I was. She slept at my house whenever she could. She would steal one of my barrettes, a tube of lipstick, a pen. She had lost an older sister when she was a child, a sweet blond-haired girl dead of meningitis at age nine. She took it out on me. As an only child, I loved exclusivity, one-on-ones, secrets, endless conversations, shared dreams, but at a certain point during the weekend I needed to be alone and very gently, I showed Lisa the door (if that can be done gently).

Lisa and I whiled away endless afternoons criss-crossing the city and dreaming of love that would need to be wearing a bad boy look, a musician if possible, since we had seen *The Doors* and wanted to suffer the way Pamela Courson had as long as our Jim was as exciting as the original model, with a beautiful deep voice, and long hair if it was up to us, and many attractive and untamable deviant characteristics. Our favourite line – "you actually put your dick in that woman, Jim?" – seemed to speak of a life of adventure. I watched *My Own Private Idaho* and dreamed of being a miserable young homosexual ephebe. Live fast, die young: I built my dream on that.

I remember a day spent methodically tearing down

Front National posters in front of my school. As we broke our nails pulling off the corners of photos of Le Pen and Mégret already adorned with graffiti moustaches, we considered our future. It was the pre-grunge era, we listened non-stop to *Use Your Illusion* without suspecting how much harm the song would do us later on (not to mention our shame at having liked the record). Lisa pictured herself flirting with Axl Rose and I saw myself with Slash in a red convertible in the Arizona desert, stopping along the road to fuck, passionately destroying our bronchial tubes and various motel rooms. The images were very clear. I remember perfectly. We just needed a way to contact them. I wrote stories but that wasn't enough, Lisa wanted to be an actress, which seemed childish. We smoked rose petals and a lot of cigarettes. Lisa puffed on a joint if the boys had one. I cleaned up her vomit. I never got drunk. We drank Malibu and milk cocktails. We decided to die at age twenty-seven, I wasn't sure who started it, probably me because it had been on my mind for a while. We wanted to die on July 3 like Jim Morrison. At first I chose the end of January because I was in love with O. who was born then, but for Lisa, the date made no sense, I hadn't even introduced her to O. because I was afraid she'd help herself to him the way she did with my barrettes, lipstick, and pens, she'd appropriate him to be a little more me. I began to distrust her. We saw *Single White Female* together and I kept her at a certain distance. In any case, I dropped the date of O.'s birthday, though he was a singer with a deep voice and magnetic hips, for the more universal historicity of the dead icon. Morrison would be our guide.

On July 3, 2007, we would go to Castellane, a pretty village where my father once took me for vacation (it was known – though there was no relationship – as a place where a cult of crackpots had built spectacular monuments to the glory of their guru). We would spend the night in a grade-B hotel with two gigolos or waiters or tourists, we would treat ourselves to an enormous banquet and an all-time sex orgy, we would try every possible drug, and at dawn, a twelve-kilometre ride in a red convertible à la Thelma and Louise to the cliff at Point Sublime, in a white dress and fishnet stockings and a wrist band, completely Courtney Love, a leap into the unknown, bodies shattered on the rocks. *Cut!*

I took photos, scouted the locations, tried out the hotel, calculated the height of the cliff. Thirteen or fourteen short years, and we would add our lives to the pantheon of the Unforgettable. Life to the fullest. Write. Live. Love. Fast, faster. Smoke cigarettes and fuck. Nothing to lose.

Lisa and I stopped being friends when we were fifteen. I tried to survive O. getting married, and she moved to another city to study theatre and live out her dream. The idea of a young life snuffed out too soon remained deeply embedded in my mind, with greater or lesser elasticity and romanticism. At seventeen I said I would kill myself at thirty-five if I hadn't published anything. My first novel saw the light of day when I was eighteen. It was not unforgettable enough to save me from oblivion. I kept trying to find a way to die in peace. I lived – but not enough – and wrote – not enough. Then, one day, I hit twenty-seven.

Deadline

When I reached that magical age, something changed. The doubt hovering over me drew dangerously closer. I had no desire to die on the appointed day, but I am superstitious and had played with fire. Something beckoned me toward what was volatile and precarious. The love I was afraid to lose – an unhealthy fear. Life slips so quickly out of a body. I had seen it happen. First my grandparents, the women went quickly, without a word, two grandmothers gone like two body blows. My grandfather, the one I knew, wasted away for four years before leaving us completely. I saw their dead bodies, their faces that had stopped belonging to them. After, I volunteered in an old folks' home so as not to lose touch with old people, not to forget death, perhaps I wanted to get accustomed to it (though what you get used to in those establishments is the smell of piss). I met someone special there, an old lady, Delfina, a toothless Italian who had had a hard life, buried her husband, then her son and grandson, and who loved me like her last and best friend. I showed up fifteen minutes late one day and saw her dead, too. I never forgave myself. I remember her rebellious look, her sense of humour, and how she thought I had pretty teeth.

At age twenty-seven, I developed a dread of death. That was something new. Maybe I finally understood what the meaning of July 3, 2007 was. That date, a little too soon to die, we can agree, was an adolescent cocoon I used to put off a more precocious death. Who would dare threaten me with early death when I had already agreed to sacrifice two-thirds of my life expectancy to the glory and beauty of the act, to the most naïve and worn out romantic proposition?

In January of 2007, fear began to exercise its slow, sure embrace. The first time, it happened on the road. Since I never got my license, I always sat in the death seat. My parents had driven late into the night. My mother was a stressed driver, I absorbed her tension in an act of empathy, like a rhizome, through her placenta. My boyfriend Jérôme drove smoothly, but he was tired because he had to cover almost ninety kilometres every day to go to work and back on a highway full of assholes and trucks. That impressed me, and I awoke every morning at six-thirty out of pure superstition to kiss him before he went off, since I was sure the day I neglected to do so, an accident would steal him from me and establish my guilt, symbolically, because I did not love him enough, or protect him enough, I had delivered him into the arms of chance.

That year I developed an intolerance for long car trips. The six-lane highways that twisted my stomach so when I arrived my whole body ached. I hunkered down on the seat, sitting as low as possible to escape the windshield when it shattered, trying to sleep because that was the most comfortable position, especially for the driver.

That year, as the anti-smoking campaigns were getting into full gear, and I was going through a pack of cigarettes a day and had been since age fourteen, I started getting this suffocating feeling. My heart pounded, I pictured the cardiac arrest that had taken my grandmother, and imagined the pulmonary embolism that had almost gotten the better of Josiane, my mother's friend who, like me, had combined cigarettes and the pill until, one night, at the age of thirty, her blood started producing air bubbles. I saw those symptoms inside my own body so clearly I knew exactly how they felt, with such accuracy that they became credible. In the spring of 2007 I underwent my first electrocardiogram, which I passed with flying colours, and my first lung X-ray. Clean as a whistle. Incredible.

On July 3, 2007, nothing happened. We raised our glasses. Miraculously, life went on without incident. That is, with the usual incidents. Yet one thing did change, forever: from then on, I could die at any time.

The Novel

There is one thing you must understand about novelists. We write stories based on our lives, and by doing so, we make sense of them, though at first they have none. Each act, each word has meaning. Like in a Hitchcock film, a close-up on the deadly weapon designates it as what it will become. We consider our lives as we live them, with that anticipated retrospective appetite to give meaning to that which, for the moment, is meaningless. We want to figure out what comes next. This is outsized pride: we are playing God.

I don't usually write "we," but I know, in this enterprise, I am not alone. I know enough people who, like me, play at God in their fiction, their writing. Who, like me, manipulate figurines that look like them down to the slightest feature. The people I associate with are atheists. Which is why they play at being God. To make up for his absence. To imagine we are not living in vain. What escapes our understanding every day will, even if it is in absurd fashion, in black and white, acquire a makeshift meaning. To free ourselves from derisive fortune. By force. And by force of self-restraint, we build puzzles out of ill-fitting stones we cut so they will form a pattern. It's reassuring. In the end, when it adds up to three hundred pages, we will achieve the fleeting impression of having made order out of chaos. Cleaned up our rooms. Understood something.

Sometimes that causes problems. I have spent whole days staking my life on a single word. If I tell that man I want to see him, what will happen? Will he want to see me, too, or will I risk weakening the hypothetical desire he might have by exposing my own? Like a chess game, think one move ahead. If I propose a time and he refuses, how should I take it? And if he accepts, then what? The clinging vines of hypotheses in the development of my plot wrap their tendrils around my throat so tightly I can't say a word. The awareness of the extreme frailty of amorous desire comes from books. Its crystallization, from Stendhal who dissected it. Its terrifying opposite, the accidental death of desire, from a Colette story called *Le Képi*, which describes a woman's joy after making love with an officer younger than she is. She picks up his cap and uses it as a game, and when she bursts into song, "playing the fool," her lover's gaze wavers and suddenly, grotesque in the mirror of his eyes, she realizes she has gone too far, and irremediably love dissolves. The young man will not return. She will protect herself with superficial dignity that scarcely conceals her shame. The humiliation of having destroyed the magic. That verdict made my blood run cold, and when I stood before the man I had been thinking of, I was too afraid to speak or act, terrified of making a mistake. I sank into the infinite reverie of the sum of all possibilities, which never delivers disappointment, never encounters the rub of skin. When you are God, you are not a man. Or a woman. Or anything else. You are pure consciousness. Because it does not exist, such pleasure is infinite.

It is here, is it not, that the truth resides: being the God of books shapes your mind so completely that it becomes untenable not to occupy the same role in life. How can you agree to accept not knowing ahead of time the meaning and becoming of things? When my parents named me Claire they took a risk. I heard this story all through childhood. My name was Claire but at birth my face was red and my hair very dark. For the first six months it stayed dark and the neighbour lady said, You should have called her Brunette. After a while my hair fell out and when it grew back it was a prophetic, miraculous blond colour. Nature wanted to give the last word to my impassioned parents who could thumb their noses at the neighbour. Do you see those green eyes? And that pale skin?

It's easy in a book. I dream of a graceful heroine, calm of mood, as patient as virtue, I decide to call her Constance – and *voilà*, that's who she is.

Pain

Every day I try to give meaning to events that have none, at least not yet. I'm short on patience. At first, when I moved to this country, I was unhappy and didn't know why I'd come here. I started having pains all through my body, I began to think that maybe after what had happened in the other country where my life had fallen apart, I had moved here to die, and that was the significance of the pain. I assigned it a fixed meaning so it could not take me by surprise at a bend in the road. I was convinced I would die here, and before the illness could take a particular form, I invented it. I invented it to be its author in case it did exist, that way it would not pounce on me, it would be my creation. The illusion of mastering it. It would do me less harm, for it would not be a shifty animal infiltrating me from behind. I gave it a name, or almost, I located its sources and symptoms. Everything was logical and fit together.

Pain is real. You don't invent pain. Yet it is the key to hypochondria, pain is as much the agent as the object. I am acted upon by it as much as it is by me.

I am not pain's fool. I know myself. Even as I fit together my symptoms to make an implacable puzzle, I know full well it is my invention. I know, in all likelihood, that the illness is a creation of my mind. To denounce it as such would put me at its mercy. By cultivating it, I keep it on a leash.

A Fashionable Illness

December 2009. For two months I had attached my hypochondria to the Type A flu virus. It had not killed multitudes, though I did hear that one of its victims was the lover of a French singer who had cancelled her concert in Prague. The French embassy there provided me with an excellent opportunity to throw fear to the wind. A group vaccination session was organized for Saturday and Sunday in the gym at the Lycée Français, just for us, French citizens living in the Czech Republic, who would not have had that privilege back home. I decided to get vaccinated and free myself of my fears. I would taste the delight of not being afraid of anything. As the date drew near, my enthusiasm wavered. My old Prague earache had returned, I started an allergy treatment, I was feeling feverish, and did an internet search on the side effects of the Focetria vaccine that France was offering its expatriates.

Very frequent: pain, induration of the skin at the site of the injection, redness at the site of the injection, swelling at the site of the injection, muscle pain, headache, sweating, fatigue, malaise, shivering.

Frequent: bruising at the site of the injection, fever, and nausea.

Infrequent: flu-like symptoms.

Rare: Convulsions, swelling of the eyes, anaphylaxis.

The side effects, I learned, are potentially more severe if a subject who is already ill receives the vaccination. The idea of getting injected with egg white and shark liver oil and a dash of dead H1N1 flu virus made my blood curdle. On the way to the Lycée, I thought of Sarkozy who was afraid of needles and my girlfriend A. who passed out every time she had a blood test. I pictured myself fainting dead away as the vaccine entered my body. At the gym, a lot of familiar faces – my courage returned. I stood before the doctor, he looked into my throat, and said in his Czech voice, soft and definitive, "No good for vaccine." He asked me what medication I was taking and shook his head. "No, sorry." I felt life flow back into me, like someone who has received an exemption from military service. I could have kissed the doctor. Then, little by little, the original fear rose up again: I could actually catch the flu.

Abandonment

Superstition is a double-edged sword. As we are using it to defend ourselves, it is hacking away at our fingers. The danger it wards off is theoretical, but the wounds it inflicts produce real bleeding. I have nothing left but stumps.

My father, a true man of the theatre, has a saying, and I have heard it since I was a girl. The actor who does not have stage fright before going on will catch it during the show, and his performance will suffer. I made that motto my own when, as a child, I took to the stage, and later I applied it systematically to every situation. It justifies my anxiety; better still, it conjures it. If I am not afraid, the fear will lodge, perfidious, in a secret place and will await its hour to spring and take hold of me. At the very worst time, of course. The danger is enough to dislodge fear and bring it out. I create a form of exacerbated, fabricated, self-imposed stage fright. I feed my own insecurity by cultivating doubt. Everywhere, in my life in society, the fear I do not suffer from sets off the fear that will torment me.

That mantra, born of the theatre, can ruin your life offstage. It has its equivalent in emotional life, and was also transmitted by my father. It comes from a quote by the French novelist Marguerite Duras, I don't know which book. I don't even know if it's just a paraphrase, so I will repeat it the way I heard it. "What sign warns you that a great love affair is about to end? Even when nothing, on the surface, would keep it from lasting forever?" In love, you will know no comfort. Everything that might reassure you will set your nerves on edge, and the feeling of reassurance that words of love can bring, and that the act will seal, contains its own negation, its morbid impulse, the supreme doubt that insinuates itself at the very moment it seems to have been overcome. Love must be impossible to last. That is not only a romantic concept, it is the conviction at the very heart of my being.

When I met Jérôme in 2000, there was a lease on our affair. He was supposed to go to Canada six months later and spend a year there, and I was living in southern France. A year and seven thousand kilometres seemed like infinity. The expiry date put a terrible, absolute pressure on our love, bringing with it an impossibility that made it precious, urgent, extraordinary. I didn't know it, and learned only that spring, but a second obstacle had joined the first: a woman was waiting for Jérôme to return, a woman he had given up on romantically, then gone back to several months later. Their union put an end to the beginning of my love. The months went by, they broke it off, and he gave up on Canada. As summer began, nothing more stood in our way. For the first time, I was happy, I trusted him. On July 5, Jérôme left me.

After that came several months of a floating relationship that offered some contentment; it seemed to promise a future. I decided to keep his camera hostage. I wanted to make sure he would return. There was this object, the most precious one he owned, I held onto it with all my might after trying to hold onto his body as he pulled away from me. He left me the camera, though he did come back for it several weeks later. Then, once Jérôme had gathered up everything that belonged to him, when nothing but desire could have motivated him, he returned one evening to stay, and we shared ten years of our lives together.

Today, when I wonder whether the man I am thinking of is going to call, I consider the objects he left with me, and flatter myself thinking they are like a treasure that means he will return. I know nothing can make a man come back when he does not want to. My hostages have no other function than to calm my fears.

I have a collection of magical objects from people whose affection has comforted me, who have helped me live. A hand embroidered pillow from Monika, in the grand Hungarian cursive style, that she gave me the day before I left for Prague. A pair of silver earrings with a Mucha motif, a gift from my students in my writing workshop. A knitted finger puppet, a little lion, also a present from Monika, that she called "Leon the Brave," designed to give me strength when I have none. My maternal grandmother's engagement ring that never leaves my right hand. A butterfly-shaped panel of stained glass, a gift from Marketa, a miniature of the Bayterek Tower in a glass globe brought back from Kazakhstan by P., a sign stating "21 means 21 we ID" stolen from a bar in Missoula by Michel, a large number of cameos from various places, a CSN noise-maker handed out by demonstrators in the spring of 2012. A teddy bear stationed on my bedside table. My paternal grandmother's clock, with this 1986 certainty from a *Paris Match* spread: Bernard Laroche did not kill little Gregory. Immortelles my mother picked in

Corsica. Multicoloured agates beach-combed in Percé. They are related to no one but myself, and the splendour of the landscape, which is why, perhaps, they are more reassuring than the magical objects, their power depends only on my own. When I look at my index fingers, their curved form reminds me of my father's fingers and that gives me strength. I summon my benefactors whenever I need them. When they are near, close by, within me, I know they will not abandon me. I possess them, they are the extension of my hand. Not them, but their essence, the metonymic magic of the talisman that connects us.

Identification

Apparently, yawning is the measure of empathy. If I yawn in front of you, will you yawn back? Maybe empathy means knowing how to put yourself in another person's place. That happens, so they say, through the use of mirroring neurons that let us interpret other people's expressions and move them into the field of our own affect. There are two operations involved in empathy: 1) imagining what I would feel if I were the other person, and 2) imagining what the other person feels.

From a certain age on, we are generally able to carry out these two operations with varying degrees of efficiency, which is one of the conditions of living in society. Empathy can also help in the theatre and with novels. But there are situations or, more to the point, subjects that set off such emotional intensity in the brain that step #2 is completely obliterated. For the hypochondriac, hearing the story of someone's illness will produce only panic, and he will try and fight it by refusing the conversation. Not that I don't feel bad about the sick person, or the one who narrowly escaped death, but my compassion is planed down to its simplest expression by excessive identification. I remember Marie telling me about her first symptoms of multiple sclerosis. The black spot in her eye. Then complete darkness in that eye with no advance warning. Immediately my own eyes felt dry and zigzags of light striated my field of vision. I remember G.'s father's swollen aorta that gave me stomachaches. I remember the sharp pains that tormented me, I struggled to cover them up, and was ashamed of myself. I practiced avoidance, I changed the subject of conversation, I found excuses to slip away, I felt myself gasping for breath, my muscles tensed up, I had to get away fast to keep from catching – not the illness – but the symptoms, at any moment. There you go, thinking only of yourself, I mortified myself for my insufficient generosity, for being so self-centred. The truth is, I wasn't thinking at all, I was busy incarnating what the other person was describing, spontaneously and simultaneously. An actor could not have done better. Panic throws me into the massive internalization of the other person's story, as long as it connects with the objects of my own anxiety. I suffer from the same symptoms but for no real reason, and can't feel compassion for the person experiencing the pain in all its implacable reality. I am such a good audience I make the other person disappear and take over his life.

One time, I was having lunch with Helena. I had broken up with Jérôme a few days earlier. At one point in the conversation, Helena told me, without any special concern, that she had no idea whom her husband was having lunch with. She never asked him. I had a panic attack, the reminiscence of my own worries, a torment that had lasted ten years. Then, immediately, a sigh of relief because I did not have to concern myself with such things anymore. That was the only benefit of our breakup: a default peace of mind that allowed me to have lunch with no concern.

Medication

Fear is an illness that has a remedy. Anxiolytics treat fear in cases where fear has no basis, no legitimate cause, the result of a deviant mechanism. What is called Lexomil in France is called Lexaurin in the Czech Republic and Lectopam in Canada.

No doctor in France ever prescribed me Lexomil. And I very rarely swallowed a Czech Lexaurin. Its efficiency put me off. The fear does not disappear but is tamed, it levels off. I have perfect recall of the way I felt the day I went to meet Jérôme at the Café Louvre a few months after we separated. The tears welled up in the streetcar as it crossed the bridge over the Vltava, I took a Lexaurin to keep from crying, the way I did the other times I saw him. The emotion was still present, but locked away in a more acceptable room. It would not overflow. I could not judge its depth nor scrape away at its bottom in hopes it would disappear. It would remain, mute, beyond tears, a purulent wound that would not open, one I would bear during the coming hours that would seem as long as months. It was not intolerable but it was present, drawn out, a form of whitlow, an edema. I picture myself across from him in a booth at the Café Louvre, the terror of spending the rest of my life without him, unable to cry, having been to the consulate where our two files were physically separated after our breakup, where I nearly burst into tears in front of the employee who executed the act. On the way out, I took a Lexaurin to avoid making a spectacle of myself, so Jérôme would not be sadder because he wasn't taking any. I took it for both of us, to help us face the moment. But not crying was monstrous, against nature. And once I was there across from the billiard tables in the red velvet of the third floor of the Café Louvre, the situation seemed so desperate it demanded tears, it was the least I could do. I was mad at myself for being unable to cry. It was like a handicap.

Medication that fights fear does not treat our awareness. It only blurs the symptoms. I suffer from asymptomatic anxiety that might get me in the end, but not right away, not today. Today I am a ghost moving forward, ordering a coffee in a voice that does not even tremble.

If that doesn't work, increase the dose.

Apricot Seeds

When I left for Prague, people said to me, whatever you do, don't get sick there. The implication? The Czech healthcare system was a lot less generous than ours. I lived in Prague for three years without healthcare, without insurance. I saw a lot of doctors during that period, careful not to let my everyday problems (often psychosomatic) get worse. No doubt it was a way of filling my days with shadow figures since I had no happiness. The ghosts within are always the most faithful.

My stay was coming to an end; my departure date had been set long ago. It was summer. The hardest part behind me. I had survived three years of living in Prague, the collapse of my love affair, sadness, and respiratory allergies. I was going to meet Caroline at a sidewalk café in Prague 6. I stopped off at Country Life to buy something to nibble on, I knew our rendezvous would go on and I would get hungry. I figured I would buy some almonds, hazelnuts, or cashews, but then I came across a curious offering: apricot seeds. That was different. I vaguely remembered my father or grandfather cracking open apricot pits to eat the seed inside.

The conversation was lively, we had two drinks each, the café was pleasant. I ate half the bag of seeds, seventy-five or eighty pieces, they were a little bitter, but they filled me up.

When I got home, my stomach hurt a little. Out of curiosity I Googled "apricot pits" to find out what their virtues were, but also because I remembered a vague warning from childhood about their bitter taste. I didn't have time to mull over the danger. Google's lead item was a warning about poisoning.

My cheeks heated up and my heart began racing. My limbs weakened when I read that apricots seeds contain cyanide. Eating sixty of the kernels over a short period of time could prove fatal for an adult.

I ran to the bathroom. I tried to vomit but I don't know how. I jammed my fingers down my throat. I did my best. My face turned red, and I had to stop when my eyes started to pop out. My cheeks were streaked with blood. I called P. who called the Prague Poison Control Centre. And my father who called the one in Marseille. Both issued the same command: go to emergency. Marseille added, *Don't worry, we have an effective antidote now, she won't need to get her stomach pumped*. P. told me he'd come and get me. He drove clear across Prague, and when he arrived I was waiting on the sidewalk, trembling, hanging in mid-air, I sat down in the car, thinking I would faint, but I don't know how to do that either. I hovered at the edge of consciousness as he went through red lights. He took me to the hospital near Charles Square. We didn't go to emergency, he found the right department immediately. They took my blood pressure: 160, though they wouldn't say if it was fear or poison. When I explained, and showed the package, and what was left in it, three nurses sat me down, one on either side, and the third stuck a tube down my nose. I didn't see it coming, they didn't warn me, I wouldn't have let them do it, I would have fought, but they were holding me down, my nose was bleeding, drool coming out of my mouth, the oldest of the nurses pushed the tube in further, and I started throwing up. I screamed at P. who was standing in the doorway *Don't look at me!* He turned his back.

Later I had to drink a glass of salt water to vomit some more. I spent the night there, in a double room facing a pane of glass, under surveillance, with sensors on my chest, and a clothespin at the end of my index finger. Sometimes my heart would begin racing again and the machine let out a high-pitched alarm that woke me, was I dying? I tried to say in Czech, *Jak rychle?* – how fast? I remember how the room smelled. P. came back very early the next morning. If it was morning, then I was alive. Great happiness. I had won. I never knew if I was really in danger. P. contacted the company that marketed the apricot seeds. He got them to reimburse my night in the hospital. And indicate on the package the suggested limit: seven kernels a day.

They say eating seven kernels a day helps fight cancer.

I never touched the stuff again.

And I respect the best-before dates on yogurt.

Vertigo

When I was a little girl, and stood at the top of a staircase, I would picture myself falling. The vision was excessively clear. In Prague, the giant escalators of the subway reawakened those nightmares, the memory of department stores where my unsteady grandmother feared falling and held my hand so tightly her fear ran from her body into mine. I dreamed of the escalators at the Nice-Étoile shopping mall, intolerably steep and fast, we used to take them to the Fnac store. In Prague I got used to the fear of missing a step, especially on the way down, I became a practiced veteran, this new city was a treasure-house of challenges to help me triumph over my childhood terrors. My first days in the Prague subway were torture. Then it became a habit, as it does for everyone.

The sudden onset of vertigo is a pathological reflex related to survival. A photo of me from behind on the aerial ride at the Prague zoo, my feet dangling over the abyss and my arms gripping the safety bar, demonstrates my reckless need to put myself to the test. Jérôme insisted we go on the ride, it would have been a shame to miss the Little Africa park that overlooks the zoo. But as we prepared to get on, I cursed Jérôme, and hardly opened my eyes, my muscles set of cramps – with the fear of what? Of dying! Yes, dying! Confronting your fears in hopes of overcoming them moves first through shame and ridicule, and the look in the eyes of your fear coach is never benevolent enough, his good intentions are always subject to doubt, their value must be weighed. Are you making me do this for my own good, to make me stronger, or to laugh at my weakness and establish your superiority?

Two years later I went back for a visit with my mother, and I was the one who said, *Come on, let's go on the ride, you don't want to miss Little Africa, there are giraffes, they practically run free, you'll see*. I watched my mother grip the bar tightly on the seat ahead of me, and recognized myself in her tense but generous hand, the way she summoned all her strength to please me.

In Montreal, my first apartment was on the eighteenth floor, downtown, at the Hôtel du Fort, the only smoking floor, then I moved to the place that is still my apartment, across from La Fontaine Park. At first I wouldn't venture onto my balcony, loaded as it was with suicidal temptations and the possibility of accidents. The owner's kids were there the day I visited, and watching them run to the railing made me break out in a cold sweat. My father slapped me for the first time (and maybe the only time) when at the age of two I tried to climb over the balcony rail on the fifth floor. I must not have forgotten the lesson.

When I first came to Montreal I started suffering from dizzy spells when I went outside, which had never happened before. They must have been caused by my cervical vertebrae, strained by the heavy bags I carried down the endlessly long streets, since all the streets in Montreal are longer than the longest street in Paris. I felt unsteady. I didn't fall, but the constant fear of falling is exhausting.

I went to see osteopaths. One day at the clinic there

were three of them, two students and their supervisor, one at my feet, one at my head, while the third placed his hand on my solar plexus and said, *You can cry if you want to*. The time it took to register surprise, and refute the idea – no, not at all – a river of tears was flowing from my eyes, all my locked-up nervous tension, I cried peacefully, out of exhaustion. After crossing the ocean at the speed of light, I said to myself, *Vertigo is the least you could get. The least virulent affliction.*

On the Plane

He asked me if I was afraid of flying. I said no. But during every take-off, I examine the progress of my life so far in case it suddenly ends there. The exercise is demanding, since I do a lot of travelling. He told me about an Italian woman whom he had sat next to on a flight, and who confessed to bursting into tears every time the plane left the ground. My mother used to do the same thing. But the Italian lady, he pointed out, took the plane every week.

It was my turn to fly the next day, dreading that the heavy snowfall the night before would postpone the flight. We boarded the plane on time, though we had to wait for a few late passengers, since weather conditions had played havoc with the schedules. The crew opened the doors for the latecomers. The security announcements were made again for their benefit. I was sitting next to a friendly student from the Congo, and behind an impolite American dressed like Kanye West. The authorities spent an eternity deicing the plane. We ended up leaving two hours late. Once the takeoff was executed safely, I was hungry and thirsty. After an hour flew by with no incidents, I tried to seek refuge in an unconvincing sleep as I waited for the meal to be served. Suddenly the subtitled Woody Allen film was interrupted by an announcement from the cockpit. "Ladies and gentlemen, we took off with a malfunctioning computer, and the backup just went down. We can't cross the Atlantic in manual mode, so we are going to return to Montreal." Several more announcements followed, bringing the contagious beginnings of panic. "We don't know what will happen when we arrive in Montreal." "Do not be concerned by the presence of emergency vehicles, that is standard operating procedure." "We will distribute customs forms in case you need them, but we are not sure that will be necessary." And so on.

I looked at the screen in the seat-back in front of me. Our flight path was displayed in real time, with our turnaround above La Malbaie. I launched into conversation with the passenger next to me to get my mind off the disaster, he was just as happy not to return to Kinshasa at Christmas, he was afraid he wouldn't be able to leave again. A little girl a few rows away started screaming that she had to go to the bathroom. The flight attendant kept telling us to stay put, since we did not have enough information about what might happen next.

I took a photo of our plane's trajectory. My Congolese seat-mate looked out the window at Montreal in its winter coat and said it was pretty all the same. I thought, *Okay, if you say so, not a bad place to die.* Then I thought about the love affair I had left behind, and how it hadn't had the chance to really get started. A shame – I would never know how it felt.

We landed. I was so relieved I had only one thought: get off the plane and find something to eat. Maybe go back to my house and spare myself Christmas with the family and its melancholy menace. Maybe even catch up with the man who said he was sad I was leaving. "Ladies and gentlemen, please take all your personal effects before leaving the aircraft." Then, as we were standing up, putting on our coats because it was cold out, moving toward the front of the plane, we were told, "Ladies and gentlemen, we are now asking you to go back to your seats, the maintenance staff will perform the necessary repairs and we will depart in about thirty minutes."

I was angry. I returned to my seat reluctantly.

"What if I don't want to depart in thirty minutes?" I asked the flight attendant.

She was taken aback, and called over the flight crew chief, who sent me to see the captain. The sheriff standing by the cockpit door spoke English. He didn't answer when I asked, "Are you going to force me to stay on this plane?"

The captain appeared. "Don't worry, we won't leave unless it's completely safe. I have twenty-three thousand hours of flying experience. And I have kids at home."

"Your life is in your hands. But my life is in your hands, too."

"What exactly are you afraid of?"

"Dying!"

They sent me back to my seat to think about it, and make my decision with a cool head. From what I understood, if they had to take the time to remove my suitcase, the plane wouldn't leave. By the time the flight attendant came back to ask what I'd decided, I had dried my tears. She gave me a maternal smile.

"The worst is behind us, you know."

"You don't know if that's true or not."

I thought about God. And the Kieslowski film, part of the *Dekalog*, "Thou shalt not have other gods before me."

The story of a scientist who measures the thickness of the ice before allowing his son to go skating on it. The ice breaks anyway, and the boy drowns. The flight attendant didn't push it. Maybe I had succeeded in sharing my fear with her.

The Heron

I was ten years old. In my theatre class my father had us work on La Fontaine's fables. I didn't like them, they seemed simple-minded and childish, my father had nourished me on Pirandello, Arrabal, and Duras whose provocative writing was more exciting to me. When he tried to convince us how important the fables were, I paid little attention. *The Animals Seized with the Plague* seemed too obvious for words, practically a piece of demagogy, *The Fox and the Crow* out of date now that ultra-liberalism had turned deceit into a shared value (especially on the French Riviera where I'm from), *The Ant and the Grasshopper* outrageously Manichean. The fables bored me, all except one, and that one made me cry. Amélie recited *The Heron*, and my father coached her to cry, too, he must have explained to her the utterly tragic nature of the fable, and that sense of tragedy, which I understood in some vague way, sent its roots into me like a fate I could not escape.

On the banks of the river, the bird turns up its nose on the big fish because he is not hungry. Then he refuses a tench because he is waiting for something better, then a gudgeon because it would be a dishonour. "For all that, said the bird, I budge on." But because he turned away the gudgeon, he will now have to eat a slug, because at last he is hungry.

I remember Madame Lamontagne, an old lady who

would show up at the theatre just as we were about to close, looking for a handout from my father. He would take pity, and help her out sometimes, and escort her back home. Madame Lamontagne, who was poor and old, had once been rich and beautiful. But she never learned to manage her fortune, she never played her hunches, and now she was forced to sell off the furniture in her apartment, piece by piece, to survive. Her wrinkles and logorrhoea threw me into such anxiety that I ran away at the thought of her. When she showed up, I hid, I skittered off and disappeared into the bathroom, if I had to listen to her I knew I would start crying.

Each time I regretted the choices I made because they failed to bring happiness, *The Heron* returned to haunt me. The missed opportunities, the reversals of fortune, the bad timing, the retrospective feeling of having wasted your life due to a stubborn move, foolish pride, a wrong choice, a school, an airplane, a kiss, a text message, a rendezvous. Tiny things haunt you when life trails behind you with regret.

There is another fable, and I read it only later. *The Girl* tells us of a précieuse who rejects her suitors one after the other because none is handsome enough. Time passes, and they become less pleasant to look at. The girl grows old and ugly. She ends up marrying a boor, her last chance. In today's world, the fable is an example of intolerable male chauvinism.

Nodule

On August 31, 2012, my friend Thierry died in Hôpital Notre-Dame in Montreal. I had heard a few days earlier that he was suffering from an aggressive, incurable form of cancer. He was forty-one years old.

We gathered at midnight in front of the hospital, hoping that Francis would still be there, since he had sent us a message with the bad news. We cried, then went up to the fifth floor, to palliative care, where the staff confirmed Thierry's death. We were not allowed to see him; we were not family. Francis had returned home to mourn and try to sleep. He had lost the love of his life after twenty years of happiness.

We headed downstairs. I went back to my place.

There is something unthinkable about premature death. It is impossible to imagine it: ten days ago I learned he was sick, and now he was gone. Ten days ago they gave him three months to live, and that seemed so little.

For a hypochondriac, the sudden death of a healthy young man confirms the most alarmist fantasies. We can, Thierry can, and consequently I can, despite the statistics, die at any moment, from any impromptu illness.

The next morning, I awoke with a urinary tract infection. I knew the shock of Thierry's death was the cause. Hôpital Notre-Dame is five minutes from my apartment.

I went to Emergency, the way people do, especially on weekends, instead of a walk-in clinic.

The doctor I saw looked preoccupied when a blue alert sounded. "Is that bad?" I asked. "Yes." My heart skipped a beat. I wondered if, the evening before, a blue alert had sounded for Thierry.

During the ten days that were allotted me to reconcile myself with his imminent death, I saw Thierry twice. The first time he was smiling, resting peacefully, his body swollen with water from the treatments, his face pale, which is what surprised me most. He was in his underwear, it was summer, he had changed shape because he was full of water, we thought of buying him new underwear, something funny or sexy. The next week I dropped in and brought an Orangina, the only drink he still enjoyed, and an avocado salad for Francis who was caring for him, and neglecting himself. That was the last time I saw Thierry. He was sitting in the armchair, facing the door. I did not let him see me. His eyes were unfocused, or maybe it was concentration, absorbed in the act of trying to swallow, or the effort of sitting up. I stayed in the hallway. I motioned to Francis and left him the paper bag.

I had time to think of all those things during the three or four hours I waited, before ending up in a blue hospital gown on a bed. I thought of Nanni Moretti's *Dear Diary* where the character goes in for a case of pruritus and finds out he has lung cancer. I tried to look on the bright side. My nervous system was just playing tricks on me. After the tests, once I told them that my right kidney was equipped with a double ureter, they sent me for a scan. The on-duty doctor who examined me confirmed I had nothing wrong with my kidneys. On the other hand, just below my lung, a small nodule attracted his attention. A radiologist would have to be called in for a diagnosis. More time went by. Enough for some moralizing: *my husband smokes, too, you know, every day I tell him to stop. But he knows the risks involved, he's a doctor as well. We'll do a follow-up scan in six months to see if it has gotten bigger.* "If I stop smoking now, will it get bigger more slowly?"

"Yes, if it's cancer."

For four months, I have smoked only one cigarette a day, in the evening, around eight o'clock, a masochistic ritual. I put on the same song, turn my back on the splendid view from my balcony. My entire day spent waiting for this moment when, with great delight, I can finally do myself a little harm, not enough to be dangerous, and too little to be pleasurable. Just enough to be torture. Just enough to draw out the trance of dependency. I spent nights bouncing off the walls, electric dawns, responsibilities tormented me, emotions like discharges of current. I gave in to them five or six times a day, tears in my eyes, tachycardia and an egg in my throat down to my sternum, slimy and hermetically sealed, allowing no air to enter my lungs, leaving me open-mouthed and panting like a dog. My symptoms aggravated by my awareness of them and their respiratory nature, pulmonary in origin. In the Montreal subway, at least twice a day I see a poster of one or several little girls stricken with a rare disease, and accompanied by the slogan "I Am Drowning from the Inside." The words hounded me for six months. How can an ad campaign, even for a good cause, go on for six long months? Wouldn't it ever be replaced? In the subway I closed my eyes to keep from seeing the serious faces of the little girls who were sentenced to die, and who immediately gave me their symptoms or, more to the point, what I thought were their symptoms. I was drowning from the inside ahead of time. Cancer or something else would get me. Or, if nothing else, anxiety, that now had an object, small and round, a half-centimetre in diameter.

What You Deserve

(The Christian Morality of the Hypochondriac)

Thierry's death gave credence to my panic scenarios, and proved that a person can die in a few days, at the age of forty, with no warning. I had pictured myself leaving this world in five years, ten years, but not six months. Postponing the deadline became urgent.

I set myself to the task. But constant frustration reminded me of the fatal conclusion, and far from bringing me the satisfaction of control, it underscored my precarious situation. Neither abstinent nor truly a smoker, liberated neither from dependency nor fear, I lost both my adolescent carefree nature (Jim Morrison style) and the tranquil peace of mind of those who can boast of a clear conscience (my grandmother).

There is something worse than encroaching death, and that is death you deserve. I often think of Thierry who did not smoke and worked out and did nothing in the way of risky behaviour. I wonder if his clear conscience helped him go in peace. And be fatalistic about it. Perhaps there is a double layer of pain when you know you deserve death, you went looking for it. I gaze upon death as it approaches, I keep watch with an extreme sense of guilt, for I have provoked it. I smoked for twenty-two years. I abused my body, wishing only to be pure spirit. "You had it coming."

Fear arises from guilt. I am afraid someone will hit me because I was mean, or because I thought I was. If I were in the other person's shoes, I might feel like lashing out. I cover my face, though the person has made no move to raise his hand. That feeling presupposes identification, a sense of empathy. We're back to yawning again. I am afraid of receiving the punishment to which I have sentenced myself. Which is why I avoid conflict: to limit the number of people who wish me ill. Perhaps they will turn out to be right. I avoid enemies, I do not respond to them, I don't provoke them, I resist the temptation to try out my rhetorical gifts on them because I know there is nothing to be gained. If I won I would create an adversary who, now and forever, would try to seek revenge. So I keep quiet.

Sometimes the guilt has no object. Or the object is me. I started smoking at age thirteen to please a certain Philippe who was eighteen and had written in an old edition of Musset's *No Trifling with Love*, "I am stupid to think that danger comes from without" as a way of proving the legitimacy of my associating with adults on the weekends when I was clearly the youngest of the group. I found a companion in cigarettes, a crutch for my confusion. A reason not to play sports since I was no good at them, a confidant for evenings when I blended into the background, the accessory of some femme fatale.

You were mean to your body, and it will pay you back by making you suffer.

You wanted to follow your own path? You'll die head-first.

Breathe In, Breathe Out

A cigarette is not an anxiolytic. A cigarette explores anxiety, transforms worry into physical matter. It deepens emotion, it anchors it in my breast like a sigh, like the inspiration I need to drive the nail into my flesh, and fill my bronchi with the emotions that run through me — as it does I let it run me through, I allow it to crucify me. I give it all the space it needs, I explore its full dimension. I take complete pleasure. Cigarettes inject it into my blood, they incarnate it, I can experience that miracle and spit on longevity. A cigarette, by piercing my chest, anchors me in the absolute present, the *hic et nunc* experience that surpasses and conquers everything, scattering metaphysical anxiety by summoning a purer variety, pure joy, too, in the end they are more or less the same thing, as is pure sadness. A cigarette is the vehicle of intense sensation, it lets me feel in stark relief, 3-D, to the exclusion of all other considerations. When I am smoking I am not afraid of death, either that or I am tasting fear so sharply it convinces me, by its very acuity, that my life is real in the present moment, and nothing, not even the vague idea of my finitude ending in a cough, can compete with what I feel: the certainty of my existence, the sensual delight of digging the hole inside myself that life has fashioned, the proof of the moment.

Fiction

The second time, I almost managed it, no problem – quitting smoking, that is. I worked out every morning, repressed my emotions, went to bed early, got up with the sun. After the first three days I believed in it, I told myself I had become someone else, I had sloughed off my sticky carapace of melancholy just like that. You could see it in my face – almost. I lost myself in the new person I wanted to be, and furtively that seemed enviable, viable. Sadness, down for the count. Knocked out! Beaten! Vanquished. But one evening, as I was trying to figure out what to declare on my tax form, the phantom of love pushed through a half-open window. I had put that spectre behind, avoided it, while thinking I was pursuing it. Since I dismissed the last suitor to whom I could not say *I love you* because I had hurt myself too badly by saying those words to someone else, love had become a threatening cloud on the far horizon. In this life, in this country, I was chasing a ghost, and I thought I recognized him on every corner, in the threatening eyes of a tall blond guy, in the acid look of that other man, a nervous jogger, a boxer, a musician. A man who would give substance to my existence – nothing less. I dedicated myself so fully to that labour, that quest, I would never attain it, that was clear enough, but the search fulfilled me so deeply it left no room for its accomplishment. "The struggle itself toward the heights is enough to fill a man's heart," so it seems. I know only two ways of giving meaning to my life, or at least convincing myself it has one: loving someone and writing books. Books are a safety net when love falls on its face. An alternate itinerary.

I recalled love as a long stab of pain with periodic high points. Sometimes happiness comes flush with it, adds a few thrusts of its own, miraculous moments when the illusion of fusion is so strong, so alive, no matter what the next moment brings, be it sweet or saccharine, it can only be a ripping away. I have the image of an organic tearing apart, the flesh of the belly shredded, two separate pieces, one in each hand, like in a Svankmajer film. I picture an illustration of Plato's androgynes made out of Play-Doh. Because I am but one, I am now nothing at all, and the emptiness is intolerable. So, perhaps, strategically, I have found ways not to experience that feeling again, ever, even as I insist all day long that I desire it with all my heart. Maybe I do desire it. I know nothing else matters.

I have devised multiple strategies to outwit love. Like a teenage girl hanging onto impossible love because it is so practical, so secure, I replaced mine with a fiction that has given me almost as much pain, offering me, one after the other, loss, rejection, weariness, humiliation, jealousy, without ever balancing those things with pleasure or tenderness. This luxury ersatz can torment me the way a real love would. Making me dependent, bitter, and jealous, ripping away my belly though it never belonged to it. By taking love and reproducing only its morbid mechanism, it sets its trap. If you give me candy seven days in a row, on the eighth day I will cry if you hold out on me. Even though I don't like candy, the habit has become an addiction. I remember the day when, for the first time, the need drove me mad. The characteristic panic attack upon waking. It was in Corsica. I was with my mother in an old house full of woodwork, with a view over the mountains and the sea. I was waiting for a virtual love letter that did not come. I awoke and loneliness cut me in two, leaving me restless. The silence was not the silence of presence, it was absolute silence, archetypal loneliness, and its void – as hollow as an empty jug – sent back a pathetic echo.

In that dance I replay all my fears, my fear of life, my mother told me. Since I can't control anything about the other person, since I know he will hurt me no matter what, sooner or later he will disappoint and betray me, abandon me, might as well give up on him now. I keep him at a distance. I choose him for one impossible reason or another, it torments me but I maintain it, an accomplice, my drug. I wish I could die of it, and just get it over with.

The worst thing about fiction is that it offers no protection. It's not even a cocoon. Even if you believe in it a crumb's worth, it will do you as much harm as reality.

"Only What I Have Lost Belongs to Me Forever" (Miossec)

It is a great temptation to give up everything I do not have yet, the terror of what I will lose in the future, and carry it over to this side, to what I symbolically possess forever by fact of its absence, an addict to lack, the metaphysical owner of what I so badly wanted to contain, retain, whose fleeting, autonomous existence caused me so much pain I preferred to let the eel escape. In the end, in a cage, proudly exposed like the inner workings of a heart or my entrails revealed, I would capture its shed skin, its relic. I gave up on the memory of what was or what could have been, and kept only its fossil as peace. More alone and stronger, it seems, the depository of that absence, that lack that constitutes me, has become my substance.

When I read Fanie Demeule's novel *Déterrer les os* about anorexia nervosa, for the first time I understood how people move, and that includes me, from dependency to sabotage, from desire to despair. Two chapters about her girlhood describe Fanie – or her literary double – completely in love with merry-go-round rides, and then comes the despair when she has to do without. Later, the object switches to grapefruit. She enters a kind of trance when after the seventh she is told to stop. From extreme pleasure to intolerable lack, Fanie constructs the deprivation that follows. If she cannot be satisfied with a limited number of grapefruit or merry-go-round rides, and does not have the power to consume them to her desiring, she can always deprive herself entirely. That is her only control: before it happens. *Flee happiness out of fear it will disappear*, as when the man I was thinking of does not write to me for twenty-four hours. If I do not have a way to make him appear, I can always shut off my computer, throw my phone into the sea, and retreat to some distant location far from the reach of the network. Rather than run up against the disappointment of his silence as each second ticks by, I will strike first, make the decision, provoke him by my own silence, be its cause and so avoid its pain.

It is so awful when it is over that the possibility of love ending makes the experience intolerable. I spent ten years worrying about infidelity, and my lover deserting me, until I finally left him so I would not have to fear that he would slip away from me. For every passing day seemed to separate him from me, and exhausted, worn down by ten years of watchful waiting, on the lookout, no truce or letup – though there were episodes of extreme togetherness whose power to torture me was exponential once they were over – I ended up chewing through the rope that kept us entwined (enchained?) and together. It is very difficult, when you have spent ten years of your life dedicated to a love affair, no matter how monstrous its form and absolute its demands, to find something else that can hold your attention.

In this country where I live now, some of my friends believe that ten years is much too long for a toxic relationship. It wasn't a toxic relationship, I tell them, it was the love of my life. I have met women who left men after two, three, or six months because they started feeling dependent. Because they began to feel the symptoms of love to which I was so dedicated. They thought it was better to run than to suffer. I couldn't make up my mind. The feeling of well-being they were offering in place of love seemed useless.

A pretty blond asked me, "Why do I only meet men who aren't free? Married men, and fathers." I improvised a reply. *Two solutions, my dear. I'm warning you – it's a projection. If you think it's nonsense, remember, I'm telling you the story of my life, I'm not talking about you.*

Hypothesis #1: Sociological. You are thirty years old and you live in Montreal. At age twenty you met boys who were free, but since then they have built their nests, had kids, and the only guys on the so-called market are ones whose lives fell apart the same time yours did. Since they are in the minority and in a confused state, they can be found in the saddest place in the world: in front of their computers. The three or four acceptable specimens who were available last night have been snatched up by some free-spirited harpy on the sidewalk in front of a club on Saint Lawrence Boulevard, and this morning they are telling anyone who will listen that straight guys in Quebec don't have the balls. *Voilà.* That's the sociological explanation, pretty depressing because it implies that unless you change eras or continents or sexual orientation, you are going to spend the rest of your life sleeping by yourself.

Hypothesis #2: Psychological. I prefer this one because it makes you the centre of your world, the problem comes from you, which is a way of saying you can change it. At least you can try. If you meet guys who are taken, you should feel good about it. Even if you claim the contrary, deep down you would be scared shitless to start life over with someone new, because you had such a lousy time of it before, you'd rather the race be lost ahead of time. That means you can relax – or almost. If you are number two in a man's life, you can live in hopes of overthrowing number one someday. And if you are number one, the wife, the mother of the child, just hold tight and pray. At best you will manage to hold on to that title through discipline and precaution, but always playing defense is exhausting. At worst you will lose your spot to a younger, more beautiful player – unless she's not as young and less beautiful.

Stop pushing away your adulterous suitors and remember they are probably as unhappy as you are.

The Butterfly

The day after my birthday the lung specialist announced that the nodule on my lung had not grown, and for the time being it did not look cancerous. On the other hand, he said, looking uncomfortable, he wanted to investigate something else, and do a PET scan (I had never heard of that before) because my thorax presented an abnormality in the area of the thymus. The what?

My passion for human anatomy did not last past high school. I don't know what a thymus is. From now on, the people I interact with will be divided into two categories: those who know what a thymus is and those like me who had never heard of the thing until I told them. You have your choice when it comes to the organ. For the Greeks, it was the seat of the soul in the shape of a butterfly, and for others it is the human equivalent of sweetbreads (Francis got that from Thierry who worked in the medical field and knew such things). The thymus is located between the lungs, beneath the sternum, the esophagus, and the trachea. It plays a part in the childhood immune system and normally shrinks during adolescence to the point of being almost invisible to a scanner in a thirty-five-year-old adult. Except that mine is five centimetres long. The PET scan should indicate whether my thymus is presenting metabolic activity. Is it growing? Must it be removed?

I walked through La Fontaine Park after the appointment

where I learned of the existence of an unknown organ in my chest. I was expecting a water lily, like in the Boris Vian story, and here comes a butterfly. Suddenly, as I crossed the empty park at nine in the morning, I could feel the organ inside me. The chest pains and respiratory problems must be the work of this intruder. I was wondering whether it was my lungs, or stress, and now I have to reconsider my symptoms in light of this new discovery. My difficulty swallowing, my elusive self-diagnosis, the occasional shortness of breath – it must be the cause. Here we are, at the theatrical crossroads of tragic irony, the moment of revelation. I thought I was losing my mind, and instead I discover an intruder that has set up shop in my breast without me knowing. I don't know if it's cancerous or just abnormal, if it contains a disease of the immune system that will soon strip me of all control over my muscles, though it is true they have never been very reliable.

The medical staff asked me what my top muscular effort had been over the past few days. I climbed eighteen flights of stairs after the last fire alarm in my building. The lung specialist looked happy enough. I wanted to know the organic history that had brought us to this point, my thymus and me. Did it forget to fade away after my fourteenth birthday (is something in me physiologically blocked in adolescence?), or did it inexplicably begin growing two years ago when I left Jérôme and the Czech Republic? I remember a girl who was raped by her father, and her mother never knew. The mother then developed cancer of the vocal cords that left her mute. The irony, but most of all the obvious meaning, struck me when I heard that story, and almost reassured me. The interpretation I could give it put me in control of the situation. Sickness is greater than we are, it escapes our control and catches us unawares, hands down a sentence, but if we can turn it into a concept, we dominate it. If I give meaning to what afflicts me then I am in charge of writing the story of my life. My water lily must have a meaning – psychological, like in a novel. A meaning. It must be a revelation, a key. It is not acceptable to be stalked and colonized by something that outstrips my consciousness, something whose existence and name and concept I know nothing of.

Arachnophobia

Girls inherit it from their mothers, it seems, it has something to do with hysteria. An acquired vulnerability. My mother did hate spiders. And cockroaches. Sometimes we had a few in our apartment. The cat played with them as my mother wailed in fear. In summer, in the country, bugs in a variety of shapes, whose names I did not know, would slip into the bathroom, between the sheets, crawl across the ceiling, drop onto our pillows. My fear had only a distant relation with the real danger they represented. I could pick up snakes in my bare hands but I would never touch a spider. Flying cockroaches give me nightmares though they are completely harmless, while I am indifferent to scorpions, slower, but poisonous.

Insects have always possessed something uncanny, *unheimlich*. Paradoxically, the crawling variety impresses me more than the flying kind, perhaps because I have greater opportunity to contemplate them. I am thinking of the centipede that comes to stand for jealousy in Robbe-Grillet's novel of the same name. The married couple eats at a table transformed into a triangle by the presence of the lover, and when he is absent, the centipede symbolically takes his place by exhibiting itself on the white wall. The husband crushes it with all his anger, and the stain it leaves will seal the marital malaise. The centipede is an intrusive presence that cannot be eliminated even after it is killed.

For if it has entered, others may follow. The whiteness of the wall is forever sullied by its oozing corpse. Cold sweat. The skin crawls.

My father taught me how to rip the legs off grasshoppers. The stories of the clouds of locusts from his Moroccan childhood made an impression on me. I could catch praying mantises in my hands until puberty showed up.

What I hate about insects is their sneakiness, the result of their small size and, most of the time, their silence. They don't knock before entering, don't announce their presence (except for wasps and flies whose buzzing is a form of politeness), they insinuate themselves into our private lives without being asked in.

I remember visiting friends, I must have been ten years old. I had not been warned. The family hosting us had my mother and I sit on the sofa, and as we were drinking our tea and eating our cookies, the little girl pointed to a twig moving in a flowerpot. "That's a phasmid stick." Then came something like a dead leaf moving slowly across the wall. "That's a phasmid leaf." I had never seen a phasmid nor heard the word. The nature of the insect, a prehistoric chameleon, camouflaged to perfection – in other words, sneaky – but worse than that was the use these people made of them. They raised phasmids in their house, in an aquarium, and let them range freely from room to room, and their two children seemed to think that was perfectly normal. For me it was the height of perversion. Only a twisted spirit could have conceived of such a project and inflicted the ordeal on me. I spent the afternoon contrite and wary, tense on the leather couch, trying to circumscribe the presence of the various phasmids in the room and hide the disturbance they caused, my itchy skin, my panic, my hatred of these people whose house I never returned to. My mother felt an attenuated version of what I did and was grateful to me, I think, for providing a legitimate excuse to exit the premises early, and express something close to disgust in the elevator.

The fear of insects, sources of attraction both strange and disturbing, exists only in cities. In the country there in nothing strange about them, and the fear they might cause is motivated mostly by the objective danger they represent. My mother lives in the country now, and she has learned to tolerate spiders, she kills them only twice a year, when I come to visit, to spare my urban nerves. In Quebec, nature is so present, even in cities, that arachnophobes are in the minority, and my panic is considered coquetry.

The nature of the insect isn't what bothers me. A fly is all the more disgusting if you find it in your plate.

An insect does not resemble me. I cannot control it, for it is too small, or communicate with it. Its strangeness cannot be negotiated with. It is incongruous in my apartment, that is what upsets me.

Insects are incongruous and unexpected, and their intrusion threatens my privacy and security. The fear is in proportion to promiscuity. If a spider moves across my shower curtain, my nudity makes me vulnerable, and the Hitchcock scene is played out in my bathroom.

An insect is the total stranger who has slipped into my bed through an open window.

An insect is the unsuspected rival, the lover in the closet, the backstreet girlfriend who makes the cuckold revisit the last six months, or years, of his married life in light of betrayal, credulity, duplicity. An insect is that pebble in your shoe you don't feel, but your foot has become so sore you can't take another step. An insect is a scandal because we didn't know it was there.

There are two ways of fighting arachnophobia, and the terror of being cuckolded. Either leave your room open to the four winds, for then no intruder will surprise you, or have no room at all and squat in other people's places. The surest way not to fear spiders is to become one.

Hunting the Butterfly

Once the organ has been named, I can feel it. It makes room for itself inside me. My body produces pain to suit it. I use it to explain every discomfort. Even my hypochondria disappears; my butterfly has discredited it. I am not unhinged, my anxieties and disorders have an object. I may be in mortal danger, but I have triumphed.

The organ has a name now, a semantic field, a diameter, an exact location, but it can have no consistency or shape. It must remain an idea. I have never eaten sweetbreads in my life and I don't think I have seen anyone else eat them, but in Montreal they have become quite the fashion. They are all I see on restaurant menus. I have expressly forbidden my friends to eat them when I am around, I would leave the table to avoid the sight, it would be as if they were devouring me. I flew into a rage with the new chef in my favourite restaurant who made them his specialty dish. He is cutting open and searing my chest, and I run for the door to escape the smell.

In May, the PET scan confirmed the butterfly was alive. Two close girlfriends came with me, with their caring they were more worried than I was that day, they took the burden of my fear on their shoulders to lessen its weight on mine. I turned down Francis' offer to come. He remembered the day he had accompanied Thierry to the same hospital.

I was leaving Montreal for five weeks, and the lung specialist promised a biopsy when I returned. No reason to be afraid. At worst they would open up my neck like for a thyroid operation, twenty-four hours in the hospital and in a year the scar wouldn't even be visible. My time in Europe was happy. I lived a little faster than usual, under pressure from the butterfly. A childhood girlfriend, a doctor, told me she recently had a young patient who had undergone an operation for his thymus. They had gone in through the boy's side, not his neck. Four incisions. "The good thing about cancer of the thymus," she told me, "is that the whole organ can be removed, there's no chance of relapse."

I started to take photographs of my neck. The lung specialist called me. He knew I was in France. He had spoken with the radiologist, a biopsy was not a possibility because of the butterfly's geographical position: too dangerous, they could hit a vein. In the absence of a biopsy, they would remove the butterfly, poisonous or not.

We made an appointment for the day after my return. His voice was gentle, and a little too detached to be sincere. I hung up and opened a bottle of rosé for courage, then dialled the number of my first love. I had been wondering whether to call him for the last month. If I died in August, at least I would have had one last meeting. I went to the horse races with my father. I photographed my neck in the rear-view mirror. I was starting to grind my teeth.

I returned to Montreal on July 12. I saw the lung specialist on the 15th. The surgeon the 19th. For the first time the surgeon said the word *tumour*. They couldn't go through my neck, he said, they would have to enter through my side. Microsurgery, with pincers and a camera they would slowly slide between my lung and right breast. "Why the right?" "Because the heart is on the left."

I don't remember if that was the day he said, "If it doesn't work that way, we'll have to break the sternum." I started picturing myself like Frankenstein's monster, with sutures across my skin and a swollen chest. Impossible to talk it over with friends. Consolation can be offered only once misfortune has struck. The Russian roulette of my body refused all appeasement. Three weeks remained. Montreal was intolerable. Every day I went past the hospital where Thierry died and where I would be operated on. Every time I heard an ambulance, panic would catch me in its whirlpool, and my chest emptied out like a siphon. One evening I put my computer in my bag and took a bus to Rimouski, then another to Carleton-sur-Mer. I wanted to see the ocean. Another bus brought me to Percé. Its famous rock was my body on a grander scale. Only later did I think of the semantic refuge of the metaphor. As long as you can conceptualize the disease, you can master it. Forget how small you are and how you don't master anything. Or accept it as a blessing. Love the natural world so much greater than you are. I ran from one side of Bonaventure Island to the other, singing at the top of my lungs. I discovered that gannets live among the corpses of their young.

I circled the Gaspé by bus, spending the night in motels. I felt very much alive with this sword hanging over me.

The Novelist's Complex

This is the problem. When you try to give life meaning by writing books, transforming life – organic, changing, unpredictable – into a meaningful whole, you end up losing sight of it as the most important accomplishment. Step 1: life is disappointing. *That's okay*, my friends and parents and even the lung specialist reply in unison. *You'll get a book out of it.* The most desperate songs are the most beautiful. There's no consolation turning your shit into books. However, pride is at stake. Step 2: the crystallization of misfortune into anecdotes, tears into lyricism. At the Villa Medici, I dreamed one night as I was shivering with fever that my urine and saliva mixed in a plastic bottle produced crystals we would put on display at the residents' next group show. A perfect metaphor for my art: the secretions of my suffering are available to the great alchemist for use in making stained glass. That is their only value. Step 3: it is what I live for because it is the only thing I come close to mastering. I look at life as material for books. Instead of living life, taking it in, eventually feeling wonderment at what is occurring, letting the magic of the moment flow through me, I program, I cross out, like a chess player I try to ward off the blows and can't sleep unless I'm a few moves ahead. If I can't predict, at least I can ponder: if I die this summer at the hands of my butterfly, what will have been the novel of my life? Every moment this thought: if the novel stops here, will it hold up? I wouldn't want to leave this world without fair warning, to avoid the sense of shame because I could not conceal my faulty parts. I have always been ashamed for corpses, I contemplate them as rarely as possible, afraid to betray them. At every moment: what would it mean if the words *The End* were written here? What would be the moral of the story?

Life, the consistency of life, is always desperately less important than the form I give it, that it seems to take as a story. Was it intrinsically mediocre or did it become that way because I insisted on looking at it as a narrative scheme? Because I was really concerned only with "the look it might have?" Be careful, it takes a certain dose of despair to get to that point. Maybe I have become one of those actors who have absorbed Stanislavski so fully that in the midst of suffering, they glance into the mirror to check the angle of their frown. Maybe that saves them. Maybe that kills them quicker. The worst: it neither lessens nor calms their suffering. In the best case, it is simply framed, underlined.

When my butterfly announced its presence, it set off an unexpected lust for life. To persevere in life seemed suddenly very precious. The energy of the tenants of death row. I left with my computer and a notebook, but hardly wrote anything. I looked at the world. I thought of Cyril Collard, my idol when I was thirteen. "It is not my life anymore; I belong to life." You really have to be in great danger to feel that the fear of dying is greater than the fear of living. The relief of facing a fear that finally surpasses the ones you had before.

Rape

The fear of rape, pornographers and psychoanalysts know, is the flip side of desire, its rejection, its retreat. This desire is not real, it does not seek to be actualized, it belongs to fantasy, it takes the worst possible event and uses it to find form, but there is no form, only a kind of dance. It plays in the mind between image and danger, like a superstition – if you think about it three times will it happen? I remind myself not to think about it, and so I think about it. I fear it, then picture it with guilty precision. The upcoming operation will be a rape. I will be naked on a table with people all around me. How many? They will shoot a brand of GHB directly into my bloodstream. They will handle my body, I will have no will nor awareness. They will slip a mask over my mouth, lift my right arm, attach it above my head. They will palpate my breast and ribs, they will slide a blade into the skin between them. I will bleed a little, four incisions in four different places. There will be tubes and they will force them into my flesh, then a camera; they will watch the inside of my body on a screen, with a pincer they will excise that five-centimetre-long thing that has no business being there.

I don't know what they will say, or watch, what they will see, or do, what they will think. I will be there, but not there. At the mercy of their hands.

Last Things

This morning flowers were blooming on my balcony in the old chrysanthemum pot that had been empty for two years. Pretty snapdragons, red and yellow, that seemed personally addressed to me. August 11, 2013, the feast day of Saint Claire, I entered Hôpital Notre-Dame, Martine and Franck picked me up and helped me cover the five hundred metres between my place and the admissions office. I smoked a last cigarette in La Fontaine Park, then the really last one at ten at night in an inner courtyard with an ambulance attendant who showed me the way. My nurse's name was Publie. I asked for a sleeping pill just in case but didn't take it. I didn't sleep. I waited quietly for morning. The lady in the room with me told me about her post-operative complications and I felt like strangling her to shut her up. No compassion here. Just try and save yourself.

At five o'clock in the morning I wrote the last two pages of my journal, just in case. Give everything to Jérôme. The apartment, the manuscripts. Publish my texts. Tell X, Y, and Z that I love them. They can bury me in Prague or scatter my ashes at the foot of Percé Rock.

I promised myself I would learn how to live if I survived. I would apply myself. Stop wasting time. Do things in style. "Superstition pursues me, with the feeling that these lines will be my last." I write the danger I am in.

Then there was no time for more than this:

> Password: clémence447
> Computer password: 212121
> Facebook / email: melantrichova

They come for me. The surgeon explains that my operation is low-risk, a 95% success rate. For the other 5%, they will have to break my sternum. They take off my glasses. I can't see anything from the gurney. The nurse hides my feet underneath the sheet. Normally you're not allowed nail polish.

Sleep

I am very near-sighted, which in itself is like half-sleep. On the gurney, I surrender all will, I accept what is imposed on me, I accompany the steps. I am an object. A piece of meat. For years I have been trying to resign myself to that state, to being no more than that, and finally the time has come. I have not been hospitalized since I was seventeen. I let them do their work. I want it to be over fast. Put my consciousness on "sleep," halt the watchfulness that has plagued me for the last twenty-four hours, abandon resistance with muscles as slack as a stuffed animal. On the gurney next to me a woman wants to make conversation. She is very excited. She is here for breast reconstruction. She beat her cancer six months ago. She is all wound up and eager to sing the praises of today's surgery. Her operation is scheduled to last seven hours – mine only four – and they are going to take fat from her thighs and inject it into her breast. The dream of so many women. I can't make out her face.

I give in to my dream. I am in love. Maybe that's just a survival mechanism. Since I learned I have a thymus and that it needed to be taken out, I have grown attached to the man I hardly know, and who lives in my loneliness. I slip into my dream. That helps. A few people nearby are talking and I want them to stop so I can flow into the dream, my life preserver. I begin to float.

I am rolled away from the affable woman and her breast. They take me into a hallway. Three young people – a woman and two men – come to see me. They are anaesthesiologists, and they have a question. For them it is rhetorical, but they have to ask it. Would I agree to have an epidural as well as general anaesthetic? It is normally used for women giving birth. I am astonished. Why? Why do that when my operation is low-risk?

"The surgeon is asking for it. If there are complications and we have to break your sternum, it's very painful, and the epidural will freeze you. Don't worry. People are afraid of epidurals because of the danger of paraplegia, but in 95% of cases everything goes smoothly."

I'm not very good in math. I wonder what 95% + 95% make.

I don't mind dying, never waking up, I have been considering that possibility for the last month. And cancer, too. And the Frankenstein chest ever since they said the word sternum. But waking up as a paraplegic – never. I haven't had time to familiarize myself with that prospect.

The female anaesthesiologist says, "You'll have to sit up, it won't take long, you'll guide us by coughing, so we get the right spot on your spinal column." That's when I refuse. No. To sit up, participate, share the responsibility. No. I want them to put me to sleep and leave me out of this. Cough, and wonder that if I don't cough right I'll be running a 5% chance of becoming paraplegic, no. Russian roulette is beyond me.

The young man gets panicky. "I'm afraid...we really don't have a choice in the matter. Surgeon's orders."

Poor guy. You would risk paralyzing me just to avoid irritating your boss?

The woman is going to call the surgeon and tell him I don't want to. Ask him if we can forego the epidural. Meanwhile, one of her colleagues comes over and bestows a big smile on me, though I don't see much of it. She must have studied marketing. According to her, the epidural is a luxury that's not available to everyone, like the latest energy-efficient heat pump. She almost convinces me. But then I tell her there will be time for it after the operation if they have to break my sternum and the morphine isn't enough to dull the pain. She counters by saying it is a lot more practical to do it now, there will be less chance of it going wrong. I am about to give in when her colleague returns. They've called it off, the surgeon has agreed to do without the epidural. I cry tears of relief. Now you're going to knock me out good and fast and get it over with.

The usual crosscheck: what is your name?
How old are you?
How much do you weigh?
What kind of operation are you going to have?
"A thymectomy."

Finally we go through the door. Light. I stretch out my left wrist. Dazzled. Anguish diffracted through my body in microparticles. The sensuality of meat on the butcher's counter.

The King of the World

The statistics didn't lie. You survived. You open your eyes and see Elisabeth's trusting smile. You feel a sort of cotton-batting gratitude toward your friends. They are there and you are not dead. You run your hand over your chest. Your sternum seems intact. Thanks to morphine you feel nothing, or almost. You think how they scared you. Mentally you tease the anaesthesiologists: *I was right to turn down your epidural, wasn't I?* You are almost angry at the medical staff for having worried you for no reason. Then you fall back to sleep.

You are floating. Your awareness comes in fragments, moments. You look at the people nearby, the coming and going of the nurses is exhausting. The smell of shit in the bed next to you. The window left open all night to expel the stink, even if you might have caught cold. You don't tolerate drafts. The post-operative dangers come welling up inside you when they hand you a blue gizmo you have to blow into ten times an hour to lift the ball inside the tube, which makes you think of the Greenwich time ball.

After the third day, the unit is overflowing, and they transfer you to the fifth floor. They place you next to a woman who speaks English and looks very unhappy, though she is surrounded by family, flowers, drawings, gifts, and employees of all kinds – nurses, dieticians, physiotherapists, etc. She is going to be operated on tomorrow, and she is afraid. You don't spend much time with her but since she is lying there in a bad state, crying with fear, you take her hand and ask what the problem is. She has had seven brain operations. Tomorrow, they are going to put back a piece of bone to close up her skull. You tell her the worst is behind her, a complete cliché, and wonder what shape you would be in after seven brain operations.

You keep to yourself as best you can, you don't want to know what the hospital looks like. It must be full of anxiety triggers. You wear earphones all the time, and hit the morphine drip at the slightest provocation. You retreat into your dream: the man you have begun to love just a little will magically come and rescue you and carry you off on his handsome steed. The image is wonderfully helpful, it makes you want to get better. It also makes you more pleasant and amiable, more alive inside. In your half-sleep you gallop along the Gaspé beaches, over the mountains, you cross Bonaventure Island and this time you are not alone. You reach out your arm. Somewhere from the drawer of the bedside table a pink agate watches over you like a charm. The future belongs to you. This time, you promise, you won't screw it up. A second chance, practically born again, you are ready to be an example for others. You believe it totally. You don't have much choice.

They come for you, you have to start moving a little. They bring you a walker, the kind the elderly use, and you take your first steps in the corridor. You put on your slippers, you achieve the vertical position. The nurse is with you, you have made enormous progress compared to yesterday when just getting to the toilet was an ordeal. You move forward confidently. You smile. You come across the attendant from yesterday who congratulates you. You go to the end of the hall and look left, then turn back. A sign indicates the palliative care ward. You recognize the yellow corridor from when you came to see Thierry last year.

"If I Don't Kill the Rat, He'll Die"

(Samuel Beckett, *Endgame*)

Sometimes I chat with my father, for him it is late in the evening, for me the end of the afternoon, we use the magic means of communication that bring us together despite the seven thousand kilometres that expatriation has placed between us. Today Papa wrote, "Black Tomcat not back tonight." Every evening, it's been months now, my father goes down and stands in front of his building at eleven at night to feed Black Tomcat. At first the cat allowed himself to be petted. Then he turned weak and got sick. Lately he hasn't been able to swallow. My father thought he would die. Then suddenly he got better. Several times, when he didn't show up, my father feared the worst, then the cat would come back. Every time I thought it would be the last. For Papa. I was afraid because he would take it hard. That upset me, thinking of his pain. I began to reconsider the distance I put between us, it made me think of my grandmother's death, the last time I saw him cry. I pictured him all alone in front of his building at eleven at night with a bowl for a cat that wouldn't come. I imagined his pain and loved him for feeling it.

I suspect C. of using a needle to put animals out of their misery. Controlling it is a way of lessening its power. Over us. Mastering it. The hardest, I know, is when the end is near, ineluctable, yet its exact moment uncertain. *Flee happiness out of fear it will escape.* Kill the dying animal to end its suffering, yes, but also to stop your deferred empathetic pain, a torture because you can't do anything about it. What C. cannot understand is that it doesn't work for Papa. If C. decides on her own, then the relief will be for her alone as well. My father tries to prolong the life of suffering animals, while C. gathers them up, one by one, and takes them to die at the veterinarian's so she won't have to see them suffer.

There is something of the novelist's demiurgic pride in the act of putting a living being to death. Refusing to be overwhelmed by nature, its violence and absurdity. Being God for others.

Drama Queen

I will have to wait three weeks for the results, to find out whether my butterfly was a water lily. Today is August 30th, and tomorrow will be one year since Thierry died. My first time outside since the operation. I walk like an old lady, but I'm smiling. I am not afraid. If it was cancer, I don't have it anymore. That's what my brain in love is telling me, since later I will go see the man who kept me in the stream of life this summer. The sun is out. Dance music in the taxi. I have an appointment with my surgeon but first I have to have a chest X-ray. In the hall in front of radiology the patients wait on chairs, dressed in hospital gowns that gape open, revealing their backs. Most of them are men, between fifty and eighty. When they come out of X-ray and go to change, their scars make mine look like nothing. A crisscross on one man's back, from top to bottom. That's what you'll look like when they take out one of your lungs. I don't feel pain when I consider the prospect, I distinguish the imaginary pain I have appropriated from others from the physical sensation caused by my incisions. I'm lucky, I realize, I savour the good fortune of not being like that man whose torso has been all but cut in two.

The surgeon confirms my hunch. I am lucky. No cancer. Not this time. My scars have stopped weeping. "They won't even be visible on your wedding night," he smiles. I will have to have a follow-up scan in six months, for the nodule and the incisions. And another a year later. You won't get off completely scot-free. They'll go on scaring the hell out of you once a year until death takes you. Meanwhile, learn to live with your fears. Your false fears worse than the real ones.

Litost

A few years ago, Jérôme told me about something called *litost*, a Czech concept he discovered reading Kundera, *The Book of Laughter and Forgetting*. The Czechs themselves can't seem to agree on its exact definition. The word means something like self-pity, or misery, or regret. Through the filter of his fiction, Kundera makes it stand for humiliation, a low-grade sense of shame that can return, suddenly, when you are comfortably seated on the sofa in front of your TV set. For no apparent good reason, you are beset by nervous tics. You feel like slapping yourself in the face when you think of the reply you should not have indulged in, the act you should not have engaged in... *Litost* can be recent or old, those from the day that has just passed are the sharpest, but worst are the old ones you return to and ruminate on, they press into you and gain the status of personal myth. Sometimes they keep you from sleeping, they sap your ego, they are all the more tenacious because you can't discuss them with anyone, they are too embarrassing, shame makes shame worse.

Sometimes *litost* springs from some small and insignificant thing, but it begins turning circles in your mind like a mosquito you can't swat. Even when it has been forgotten, and processed, it can spring out of nowhere because of something heard on the radio, a glass you break, an accidental encounter... The sudden resurrection of a *litost* can be a handicap in daily life. There are words you can't bring yourself to speak, songs you can't bear to sing, people you neglect for the simple reason that they rekindle the unpleasant memory of a *litost* you would prefer to bury. Since I discovered that the little pest has a name, I have gained some control over it. A diagnosis is the first step toward relief. That horrible slip of the tongue, that zipper left open, that misstep, that stupid reply you should not have made, there is a name for it, a Czech name.

The fear of *litost* is not equally distributed among individuals, some people are particularly sensitive and go to great pains to avoid it, but there is only one way to preserve yourself entirely, and that is misanthropy. *Litost* is a social disease. The more contact you have with the outside world, the more you are exposed. Evenings on the town are great reservoirs of *litost*, as are work meetings, book festivals, and teaching at the university or anywhere else. Politicians are formidable processors of *litost*, I would have thrown myself out the window a dozen times if I had the record of some of those men. The same goes for TV hosts. To process *litost*, some people eat amounts beyond what is reasonable, others smoke, drink, or take drugs, still others decide that they despise the world in its entirety, while others have the ability to shrug off *litost* like water off a duck's back, they absorb one after another, all day long, and scarcely realize it, such people are humanoids shrouded in mystery, forever strange.

As I try to focus my attention on the book I am working on, I slap myself in the face, but not too hard, to try and banish the memory of that seminar on sociocritical thought where, last week, I attempted to explain to a dozen Quebec students that the slogan "we're from Marseille, and we're not gay" is a soccer stadium chant that has more to do with regional stupidity than homophobia. I quickly realized my attempt was a dismal failure, and knew it would come back to haunt me that night. The little slaps I administered myself were symbolic acts of punishment (you were an ass…) rather than ways of diverting my attention through physical pain. Which proves that, even in shame and guilt, I am much too indulgent with myself – not to mention with the machos of Marseille, homophobic through culture and not by conviction, for whom I have a certain affection, in spite of everything.

Even Paranoids Have Enemies

You need to be careful if you happen to have paranoid tendencies. First off, you think people are malevolent. That's the basis of everything. But when you've been paranoid for a while, you begin to get used to the condition, and learn to fight it. You are aware of your twisted vision of human relations, and prepare compensatory strategies. Every time a stranger on the street casts an ill look your way, you tell yourself, *That asshole, what does he want from me?* The next minute you realize, No, that's just my imagination, that person is probably charming and has no harmful intentions. You kick yourself in the butt and try and assume a sympathetic manner with the stranger. Sometimes, your first intuition turns out to be right: the stranger really is an asshole. Once his true nature has been revealed, you may get the unpleasant feeling that you've been tricked when you thought no one could catch you unawares again: you were guilty of excess trust. That's paranoia in its most exacerbated form, which often leads to naivety, or worse. In that case the paranoid's feelings are mitigated, because in a certain way, he is happy to have seen the truth. *I'm not crazy*, he reassures himself, *I was just using my intuition*. At the same time, he is irritated as all get-out because he fell into the trap, though he has sacrificed part of his psychic health so that won't happen. That narcissistic wound – the worst kind for a paranoiac – produces considerable distress. First, the paranoiac, swearing, though a little too late, that he won't get fooled again, decides to retreat more deeply into his paranoia (which, it is clear, seems less degrading to him than excess naivety), and will become completely dedicated to his disorder for a period of time. Second, the paranoiac must avoid crossing paths with the stranger on the street who does have ill intentions, since the former's aggressiveness is wound tight as a drum, and he is likely to haul off and take a swing at the guy.

Fear of Conflict

I like big men the way some small men like big dogs. As if they had the power to protect me. Maybe because my grandmother limped, or because we're not athletic in the family, or because I have no strength in my arms. I don't know how to defend myself. My defense is my sense of judgment. I don't shout, and I don't hit. I don't know how to do those things. The only conflicts I engage in are with intellectuals. If I had ever been in a situation where I had to defend myself, maybe I would have learned to, but I am so afraid of the possibility I prefer to cling to the prudent certainty of my incapacity. Behind every avoided conflict is the fear of getting hit.

When I stopped smoking, I started exercising, not to fit into an ideological schema I detest (though it is very hard to resist the North American model with its parks full of joggers), but because one dependency is as good as the next. I replaced nicotine with dopamine, to which I became addicted very quickly. My muscles, still rather discreet, are trophies I contemplate with some satisfaction.

My stepfather told us at Christmas how he was attacked by two punks when he was young, and how he sent them running with the help of a knife. The story impressed me because I knew I wouldn't be able to react physically the way he did. What I have always considered my civilized side, my cowardice, is a source of shame as I build up my muscles.

When I was eight, I burst into tears over a stage slap. The actress who was playing my mother came and apologized in the wings. She had not actually hurt me; it was the humiliation of being slapped. She had done her job well, and so had I, beyond anyone's expectations.

I wish there were a punching bag in my building's gym. I would bang the hell out of it and that would do me good. I would thicken up my wrists and toughen my biceps. I would give it a few choice kicks, too.

I used to go target shooting with a .22 calibre pistol. I wiped out my enemies with every bull's-eye. The shooting range is the most peaceful place on earth. Everyone is calm, aware of the consequences of a mistake, a false move, chastened by the noise of gunshots that remind us that death is at hand, a trigger squeeze away.

I filled out the papers for the firearms permit and took them to the police station. I signed a formal declaration that I had never been in a psychiatric hospital, which is a condition in France to get approved. I bought a regulation case, and went about choosing my weapon. Just as I was about to buy it, I changed my mind. I didn't want a gun in the house. I could have left it at the range. At home you never know what might happen. One evening, after a fight. I was worried more about suicide than shooting someone. My supposed inability to defend myself has always led me to focus my violence inward.

Rape 2

"The relation between author and reader
is like the one between a man and a woman."
— Sartre

Today I read a book. A novel. The whole thing. I hadn't done that for a while. Not that I took any great risk; I had seen the movie version a few years before. I jumped to the end, knowing that people generally do that out of the need for reassurance, to avoid being taken by surprise. And when they do, they cheat themselves out of the pleasure that comes from just that — being taken by surprise.

I learned to read late. Until I was nearly ten I enjoyed the delights of slavery: other people read to me. My actor father did all the voices from *The Famous Five*, and my grandmother sent me off to sleep with the Comtesse de Ségur. Only very recently, I understood that my fascination with the name Camille came from *Les petites filles modèles*. I went to the theatre every weekend, it was easy. When my father directed, it wasn't so easy because he put on Arrabal.

I read less and less these days. Apparently that happens frequently, it's one of the symptoms of depression, the self closes up and becomes more prudent. The person is less willing to risk being moved, penetrated by a story. I read because I have to, for my work. Part of my job includes reading what other people write. Reading with a pen in your hand is not really reading. You maintain an active mind and engage with a text that you dominate, whatever its quality, you are not really in the text, you are perched above it, it may try to enter you but you are wearing your overcoat. Whatever emotion it produces, and it may be very eloquent, you are prepared, your muscles tense, the blows to your solar plexus are not painless but they present no real danger. I read sections of books. In sections, books are almost harmless.

I read very little because reading means being entered. According to this tenacious representation: reading is passive, writing, active. Writing, for a woman, is contrary to nature. By writing I free myself from my female condition as prey, an object of siege. Reading is retreat, renouncing. I can't write and read at the same time. Most of the time, if I have the choice, I choose writing. But I can write only by processing what I have read. I choose my nourishment according to what I wish to take in. And even then, I page through diagonally, it is a protection, like contracting my perineum. I do not let things I abhor enter me, anything that might be cause for worry, what I do not desire, what might disturb me. I close my eyes to love at first sight. I don't have the time, my days are numbered and perhaps so too are the images my brain can come up with. I keep myself away from foreign scripts whose wounds I could not bear. I am wrong, I know, but I don't do it on purpose, I wait for it to be over with. Sometimes I push myself. I write to penetrate you, gentle reader, it is my revenge against physiology.

The Metaphysics of the Bourgeoisie

The characters in Zola's books have no psychological problems. They are not trying to stop smoking. Procrastination – the word and the concept – is foreign to them. No need to wonder if they will be able to work today. The existential emptiness and screaming panic that fills my smokeless days are a geopolitical symptom. I am of the era and class that has the leisure to look for meaning in life. I think of what my young friend Philippe wrote in my copy of Musset when I was thirteen: "I am stupid to think that danger comes from without." We are of a peaceful civilization, threatened neither by war nor famine, we cultivate the monsters that devour us from within. A generation busy measuring the speed of its self-destruction.

With a smile, Thomas Ostermeier said this of the former East Germany: perhaps it was paradise. We had Trabants instead of Mercedes, but we could drink. And we had a clean conscience.

I saw that in Prague, where the sanctity of a free society after forty years of Communist occupation would never – or so we thought – lead to the prohibition of tobacco in public spaces. Life is a matter of priorities, an advertisement from my childhood proclaimed. If you're wondering how you are going to make a living, you will wonder less about how to preserve your bronchi and your neurons. When you drink for courage, when you drink to stay warm because it's cold outside, you don't ask yourself whether you're putting yourself at risk of a heart attack. The same goes for ecology. In Prague and Montreal, people don't cut the furnace in winter to save the planet. When winter comes, they turn up the heat. Otherwise, they'll die.

Why would anyone want to draw out their life expectancy when, in the best case, you are whittled away to nothing, and in the worse, you die of boredom? Such arrogance to think you can extend your life. You think you're God, and not only in your books. Defying nature by preserving it, one minute at a time, from programmed disappearance.

I am of this docile society obsessed by danger from within. What I eat, what I drink, what I smoke, how I fuck, the harm I do myself. If I had some outside danger, no doubt I would be less afraid. My inner danger seems more familiar and less perilous because I own the key, the lever, the thermostat, or so I think. I used to have my small portable danger in my pocket at all times. I called it Lucky Strike. It helped me forget the other dangers not under my command.

The electronic cigarette I activate when the compulsion returns has nothing to do with the Lucky Strikes I lit up when I was thirteen. A smoke stood for carelessness, riding the Mad Mouse, the dare-devil cowboy defying God. An e-cigarette speaks of fear of cancer, repentance, rehab.

The oldsters on the bus in Nice say the only thing that will save us from decadence is a good war. They reminisce about the good old days of the war as they slip their paper into the ballot box, and when they sing the national anthem, they tell themselves that impurity comes from the other side of the Mediterranean. Hating your neighbour may well be a way, rhetorical but efficient, to keep from hating yourself.

The Power of Destiny

Destiny is a right-wing word. Individualistic like tragedy, it presupposes heroes, an elite class, divinity, it whispers to you that there is no sense fighting to change the natural course of things, it is greater than you are.

Francis told me about Thierry's first cancer, seven years earlier. He survived it at the cost of a kidney. Survival gave him strength and the lust for life. The way I knew Thierry, his smile, his body, the shape he was in, his epicurean side, his healthy lifestyle, all forged by that experience.

To survive once does not protect a person against future peril. As long as you're alive, you can die tomorrow. The trick is to forget that prospect. I am working on my Pascal-style diversionary tactics. I get high on dopamine instead of tar, and try not to pray because I know it's no use.

It is stupid to be fatalistic unless you don't have the choice.

Inventory

Now that I am bringing this inventory to a close, I wonder what made me agree to it in the first place. I tremble as I reach the end; writing is not a means of escape. Or if it is, it resolves nothing. I do not want to be displeasing and that makes me cowardly. I am afraid of dying before I've accepted death. I am afraid of living in vain. I am afraid of never being loved again. I am afraid of not really living. I am afraid my mother will grow old and die. I am afraid she will never die and I will break her heart by going first. I am afraid I thought of that man needlessly. I am afraid no one will ever stroke my hair. I am afraid of being forgotten, I am afraid of being replaced. I am afraid of losing the faces so dear to me. I am afraid of forgetting their features. I am afraid of what you will say about this book. I am afraid of the label you will stick on my forehead. I am afraid of your denial, your contempt, your condescension. I am afraid of being dismissed with a careless word. I am afraid I am handing you weapons to use against me.

« END »